D0429232

The Daughters of Ys

Written by
M. T. Anderson
Art by
Jo Rioux

First Second
New York

To T.W.
—M.T.A.

To my parents
—J.R.

Published by First Second
First Second is an imprint of Roaring Brook Press,
a division of Holtzbrinck Publishing Holdings Limited Partnership
120 Broadway, New York, NY 10271

Library of Congress Control Number: 2019938062
ISBN: 978-1-62672-878-3

First edition, 2020

Edited by Mark Siegel and Whit Taylor
Cover design by Colleen AF Venable
Interior book design by Chris Dickey

Printed in China

Penciled with Prismacolor Col-Erase in terra cotta and black.
Inked with Prismacolor Premier fine line marker in black and brown.
Colored digitally with Photoshop.

10 9 8 7 6 5 4 3 2 1

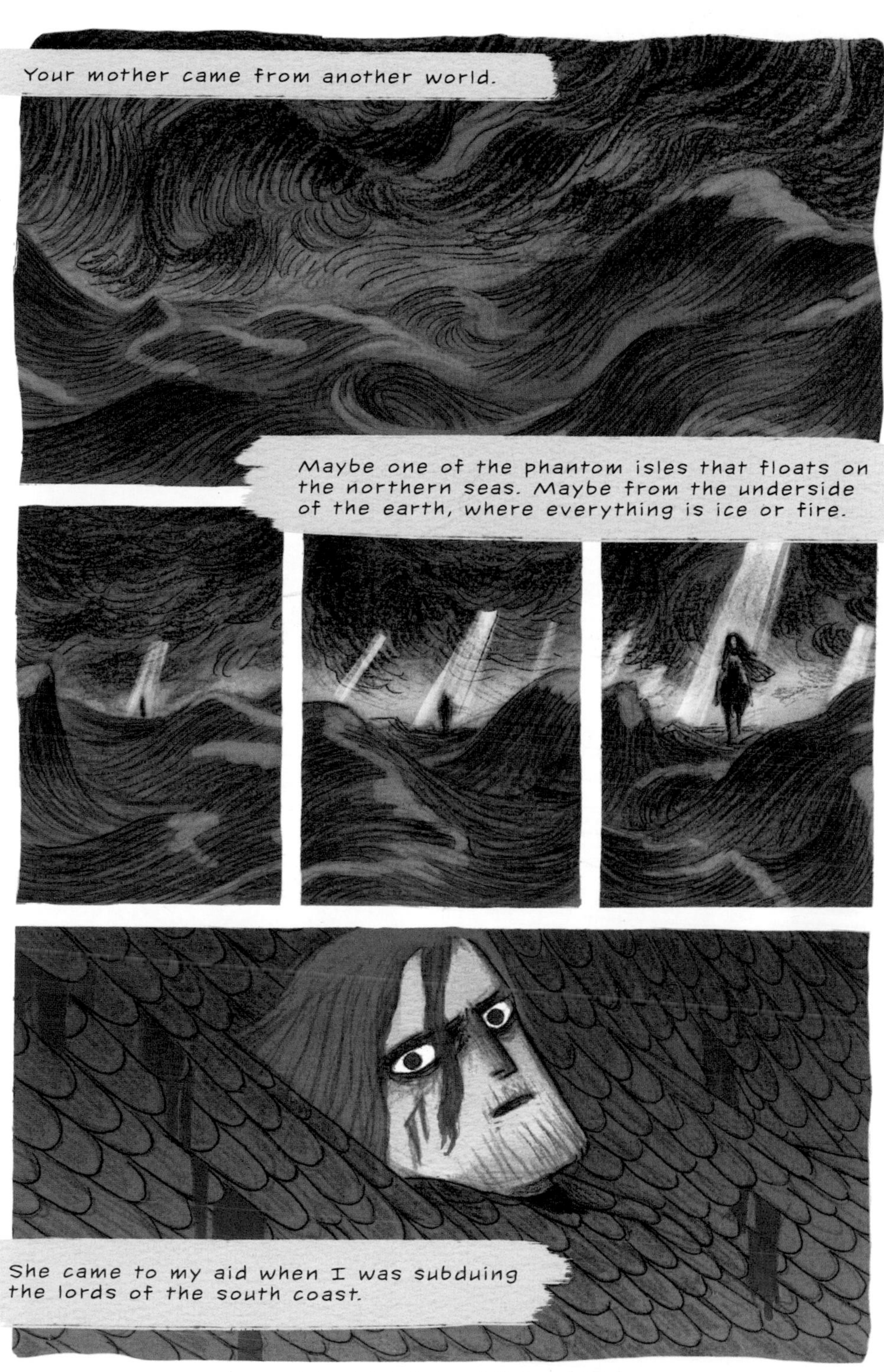
Your mother came from another world.
Maybe one of the phantom isles that floats on the northern seas. Maybe from the underside of the earth, where everything is ice or fire.
She came to my aid when I was subduing the lords of the south coast.

Gradlon, King of Kerne?

This is a strange meeting.

I have heard much about you and your warriors.
This is not the finest day for the warriors of Kerne.

I see that. Better that I change your fortunes, King Gradlon.

Madame, I would not refuse a favor.

Kill my husband with me and you will find that all Kerne thanks you. As will I.

Not easy to accomplish. I am floating in a ship with no crew left alive.

My horse's footing is sure. Will you join me, King of Kerne?

What is your name? Who is your husband?
I am Lady Malgven, and I am the wife of the Wizard Duke of Wened.
Perhaps you have heard tales of his sorcery. Kill him, and his lands are yours...

I wish to make the acquaintance of your noble husband.

REEEEEE!!
FRSHHH

REEEE
SHRIEK!!

SHLACK
THUMP

You will be welcome in my kingdom, Lady Malgven.
If you take me as your queen, you will find we will rule well together.
Take me to my capital, Quimper, at the meeting of the three rivers. I will think on it.
Make me your bride.

And I will use sorcery to build you a new capital. It will be more beautiful than any city made by the hands of men.

You will make me feel joy. You will give me children.

For you, I will build walls to push back the sea and will spin you a palace of domes and towers.

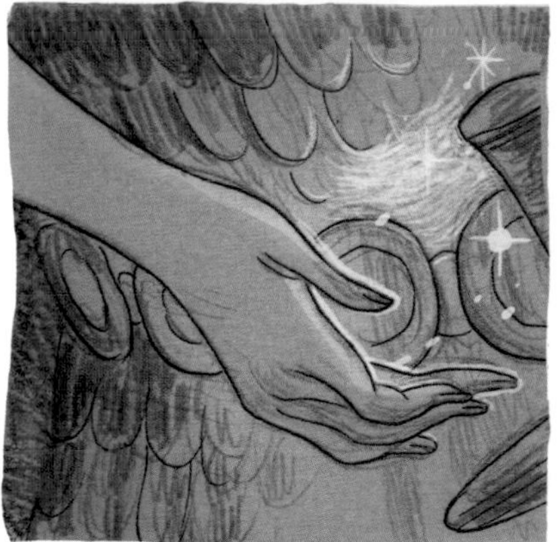

I think perhaps I am interested in marriage.

And so I married your mother.
She called up powers that pushed back the sea and made the great walls of this city of Ys, and it became our home for many happy years...

And now she's gone.

She lives on in the two of you.

Rozenn, my eldest, to you she gave her love of wild things and lonely places...

And to you, Dahut, her love of wonders and miracles.

Bid your mother farewell, my daughters. We send her back to whatever world she came from.

Perhaps the people of her faerie lineage will hear of her death and mourn for her, too.

As for me, I am lost in a darkness deeper than the sea beneath her burning body.

Why did she die, Rozenn? Why did she grow old like that, suddenly?

Maybe in the world she's from, time moves different. Maybe ten years was passing for each year she spent here.
Then she'd be a hundred and twenty. Older. A hundred and fifty.

I don't know, Dahut. Maybe the magic made her grow tired. Each time Dad asked her to build something new, she looked older. I think it wore her out.
And he kept asking her to build and build. New gardens and mirrored halls and brass spires and chapels.
And the sea monster.

It sank another English ship the other day.

There was a golden circlet in the loot. Mom would have given it to me.

Ask Dad for it. If you want it.

ROOAARRRK

SPLASH

What are we going to do without Mom?
I wonder if the Wizard Duke of Wened was a bad person. If he'd trapped Mom, maybe.

Why do you care?
Faerie lords and ladies get trapped sometimes by sorcerers.

I don't care about the Wizard Duke of Wened.
FWSHH FWSHH

Dad killed him. Maybe without any reason.

And if he hadn't, we wouldn't be here. We wouldn't even exist.
And another thing about the sea monster...
I hate the sea monster.

Who's going to run him? Now that Mom is gone?

Maybe no one. Maybe it'll go away and disappear in the Frozen Sea again.

Rozenn, we *need* the sea monster.

That's how we make the world tremble at our command.
I don't want the world to tremble. And the roaring wakes me up.

What does he even eat? Other than sailors?

The flowers still look a little scratchy. And dull.
The purple is for mourning.

Do you think Mom would have liked them?
She liked whatever we did, Dahut.

Especially if it made the princes and ambassadors laugh. Let's go pick some-thing more exciting in the hanging gardens.

I like brown.
No one comes from Rome or Samarkand to see brown flowers.

Are we of faerie blood?

I guess.

So will we age quickly, too? And die suddenly like Mom?

Uh...

The guards should have...

What? I don't believe this! Who's that? Who's this?

Life is short, Dahut. We must grasp what pleasures we can.

You don't look like you're grasping pleasures. You look horrible. You look awful.

You are awful! You're awful!
Let's go, Dahut! Let's go! Leave him!

I hate him!

We'll take your mind off your problems.

Yes. Take my mind off... my problems.

sob
sob

It's only been a week!

I'm telling you, he did.
I hate him.
Don't say that.

CRR
CRRK

What do you have in your hand?

That's Mom's!
She told us never to play with her magic things.

I'm not playing!

CRRAACK

cheep!

Ha!
Oh!

No!
pof

I'm sorry.
I'm so sorry!
I didn't mean
to hurt it!
It's still
alive.

What can
we do?
Maybe if I take it
out to the fields,
it will get better.

Let's go!

I'll go.

All right.

But I'm really sorry.

I'll see you, Dahut.

See you, Rozenn.

Mom!

There's a feast at the palace tonight, Morvech. Unfortunately. It's the equinox.

I'd rather lie out in a field, watching the stars turn in the sky.

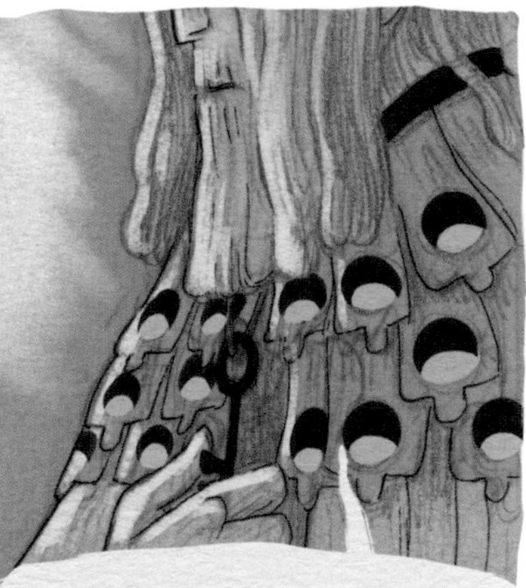
Kings, princes, merchants, travelers—welcome to Ys, famed city of pleasures.

This is our daughter, the Princess Dahut. Our daughter Rozenn will be here at any moment.
We invite you to our royal palace where you shall see many wonders.

The renown of Ys and her wealth has spread throughout the world, King Gradlon of Kerne.

All navies tremble at your name. All merchants long to travel to the markets of Ys.

The wonders and beauties of this palace have been spoken of in the far courts of Muscovy, Cathay, and the Palatinate of Prester John.

"Where is Ys? I say that there is a city more beautiful than Paris."

It is with joy that we greet
She's very beautiful.

Be careful, my prince.
She's the younger of the sisters, not the heiress.

But if a kingdom came with this girl...
There's the older one.
Oh?

You're late.
They have already started their speeches.

She's the one who will inherit the throne. Beautiful, too, but crazy.
Does she have sticks in her hair?
She lives out in the moors.

Have you met the King? Gradlon?
Also crazy. With grief. His wife died six or seven years ago.

He stays in his own wing of the palace except to conduct business and to go out on raids.
Burning down coastal cities. Looting. Capturing Saxon slaves. But his heart doesn't seem to be in it anymore.

How long would you say he has to live? Will his kingdom be divided between his daughters when he dies? Does he seem at all interested in suicide?

For your pleasure, we will now summon the tide. With this key, we control the sea and her children.

CLICK

CLACK

digga
digga
dig

FWSSHH

Oh!
gasp

Let the pageant commence! The noble children of Kerne have tamed the creatures of the deep.

SPLASH
SPLASH

Thank you for arranging this entertainment for the guests.
We need to dazzle. Your boots are covered with mud.

Princess Rozenn, Princess Dahut, the kitchen is ready with its flock of basted birds.

Am I finished here? Can I leave?

It's up to you, Rozenn. You're the heir to the throne.
These feasts make me feel like I'm choking.

Not just a hillock of roast birds. Watch.

SWIK

PSHHH
PSHHT

It's a wine fountain.
Where do they get their money?
Plundering. They have sea monsters.

And how do they harness all these monsters? All these magical spectacles?

No one knows. But behind every fortune, there's a dark secret.

If you gentlemen will excuse me, I think I have some dynastic business to carry out this evening.
My prince?

Founding a dynasty. More entertaining than it sounds.

I'll go meet them
in the morning.
The merchants.
The princes.

Let them
have fun.

And in the morning...

Phew!

Oh, really? Do you really?
Come to my tower tonight and maybe you could show me.

It would be my pleasure.
Don't get too friendly. I'm the younger sister.
I think you'd prefer Her Majesty the Princess Rozenn. She'll inherit the kingdom.

And where's she?
She left. She's a lunatic. She consorts with wild pigs.

Then I guess I'll have to make do with you.

When you come by the tower, wear a mask.

Here.

We don't want anyone to know you're visiting me in the middle of the night, do we?

The young lady has equipment at the ready.
This isn't the first time you've done this, then?

And it won't be the last. Remember that. Fair warning.

chirp
chirp

The wild Princess Rozenn.

I've heard there was a holy hermit who lives among the standing stones.

Corentin. I pass through. Sit down.

I don't want to disturb you.
The stones are yours. Your ancestors raised them.

Really? Human or faerie?

It's a quieter feast here than the one in the palace of Ys tonight.

plop

Every day the Lord gives me a fish to eat.

That's kind.
No, it isn't. It's always the same fish.

My sister and I once came to see these standing stones on New Year's Eve. It was very cold.
But at midnight, as the year changes, all the stones wake up. They pull themselves out of the ground and stampede down to the river to drink.

Once a year? Thirsty.
They would have crushed us if our mother hadn't been with us. She could talk to them.

She must have been a persuasive woman.

A bite.

Good evening, old friend. I'm sorry. I waited as long as I could.

whack

It's midnight; you had a full day this time. I try to eat as late as I can.

It's really exactly the same fish? Every day?
That is what the Lord grants me. And the fish.

Then he's almost like a pet! And you're going to eat him?

Every day I eat half of him. He will appear again tomorrow, whole and healthy. Until I catch him again and carve him up.

How can you kill him? Every day?
We live by devouring those we love. How can we help it? They're the ones within closest reach.

But you're a holy man!

And yet, here in the wilderness, I live out the dream of all of the wealthy and the powerful:
to be able to consume continually without depletion.

There's a whole fish.
Take away half, take away half, take away half, and he still is whole.
Infinite replenishment...

...Princess, how do you think the city of Ys stands against the sea? How does it acquire its fabulous wealth? There must be a price paid.

Except for this miraculous fish, nothing in nature produces bounty for man forever.
Wells dry up. Forests disappear. Fields turn gray and lifeless if sown too often.
Sea walls decay with the battering of years. Cities die. Ys cannot forever sustain its luxuries.

Not everyone has to kill and destroy!
Would to God that what you say is true, Princess.

Good-bye, my one true companion. My other half.

You murder him every day!

For that reason, I have never been able to figure out whether this miraculous fish is truly a blessing upon me from my God...

...or whether he is a curse...

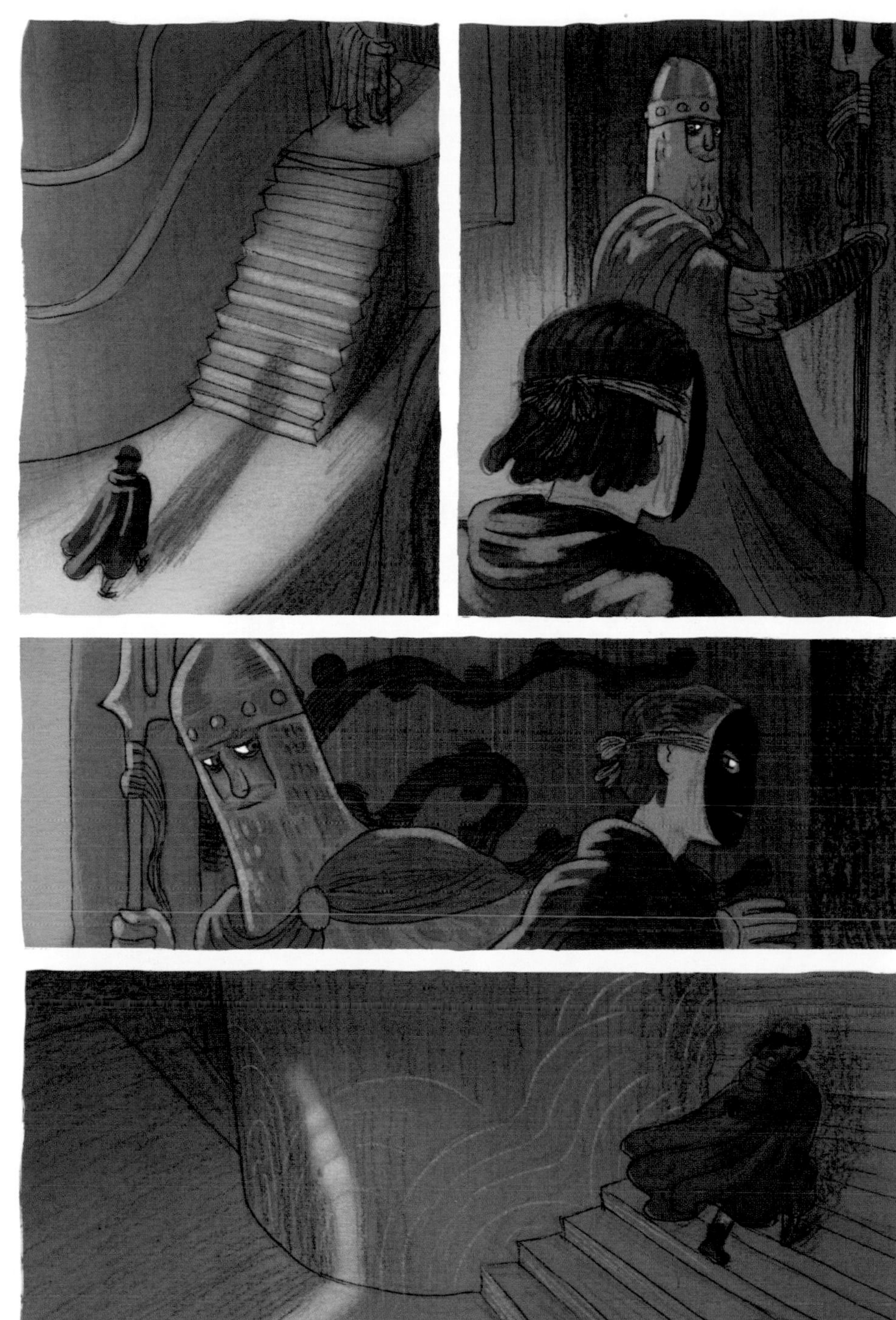

You're a surprising woman, Princess.
Life is short, Prince. We must grasp what pleasures we can.

I've enjoyed our kingdoms' diplomatic relations.

Absolutely. That was that.

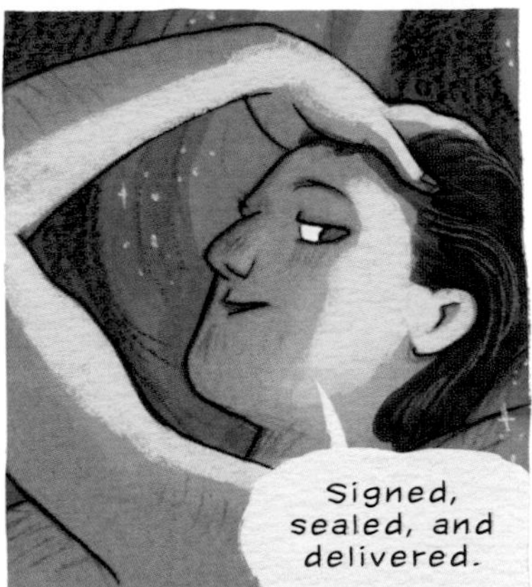
Signed, sealed, and delivered.

Wear the mask as you leave.

Don't let anyone know you visited me here.

Depending on how negotiations go today, maybe I'll see you again tonight?

Princess, the mask is tighter than it—

SKWIK

Princess! Prin—

Hurk!

SHLACK

THUMP

drip
drip
drip

drip
drip
drip
drip
drip
drip
drip

There's your payment, you bastards.

Shoot the bird and I'll skin you like a rabbit.

I didn't see you!

You saw my bird.
Didn't know he was yours.

Why were you going to kill him? He's tiny.

To give to my cat.
Let her catch her own snacks.

She's blind. She walks into menhirs.

Haven't I seen you before?
I live in a village near here. In Douarnenez. I'm Briac.
And who are you?

I'm a force of nature.

What's her name?

Doesn't matter... She's deaf, too...

King Gradlon, the prince has been missing for six days now.

The things of this earth pass away and leave no trace.

The first day, I thought he was simply off on some...adventure.
Now it is clear something has happened to him.

Ah. To whom do things not happen? Only the dead.

He isn't the first! There have been rumors that many young men disappear here!
There's something wicked going on! There have been—

If you finish that sentence, your lips will be cleaved in two as you utter your final period.

I suggest you leave in a huff.

Your...Majesty...
King of...Kerne...I humbly
take my leave...to return
to my own kingdom...

So much sadness on this earth.
And now his ship will disappear, lost at sea. The prince's parents will never know he even reached these shores.
These tragedies...

I'll arrange it, Dad.

Thank you, Dahut. You're a good girl.
For dinner, shall we have an octopus inside a roast pig or a roast pig inside an octopus?

Hurry! Hurry! If you want to make it home, then for Christ's sake, hurry!

AAAH!
ARGH!
AAEEH!!

CRASH

SPLASH

Mmm-hmm

Ocean, sweet ocean blue,
Wash me on the sands,
Toss me in your waves.
Let me be your lover,
Sweet ocean blue, my sea.

By the green, clear
waves was I born,
And when I was small,
You roared for me,
You rocked me on your
back,
You scolded furiously.
But when I stroked
your mane,
You whispered to me
deliciously.

Ocean, sweet ocean blue...
You drown ships and hearts.
Now bring me beautiful
shipwrecks,
Bring me vessels full of
silver and gold.

Bring me sea pearls
and opals,
And the hearts of
fierce men
and pale boys who—

...and every day he eats half his fish.
The fish can't be too happy with that.

If I ever rule this country, I will do things much differently than my father.
A queen should be the voice of her kingdom's people.

And I'll serve you faithfully.

Serve me what?

When you're queen, would you ever consider marrying...someone who wasn't royalty? If he loved you enough?

Sometimes old rules have to change if we want to grow.

What is this place?

It's called Our Lady of the Tempest.
All the fishermen come here.

We come here in processions from the village. We bring models of our boats and ships to pray for protection.

They're beautiful.

It hasn't been working. A lot of ships have gone missing.

What's wrong?
Nothing.

!

I feel safe with you. Like I've finally come into port.

SPLASH

Stop staring.

I do what
I have to.

Rozenn!
Hello, sister!
Hello,
sister!

Out fishing?

Yes.
Singing to
the sea?

You found a
nice fisherman.

How's
Father?

Rozenn, we haven't seen you in weeks.
I can't stand Ys anymore. All that noise and riot.

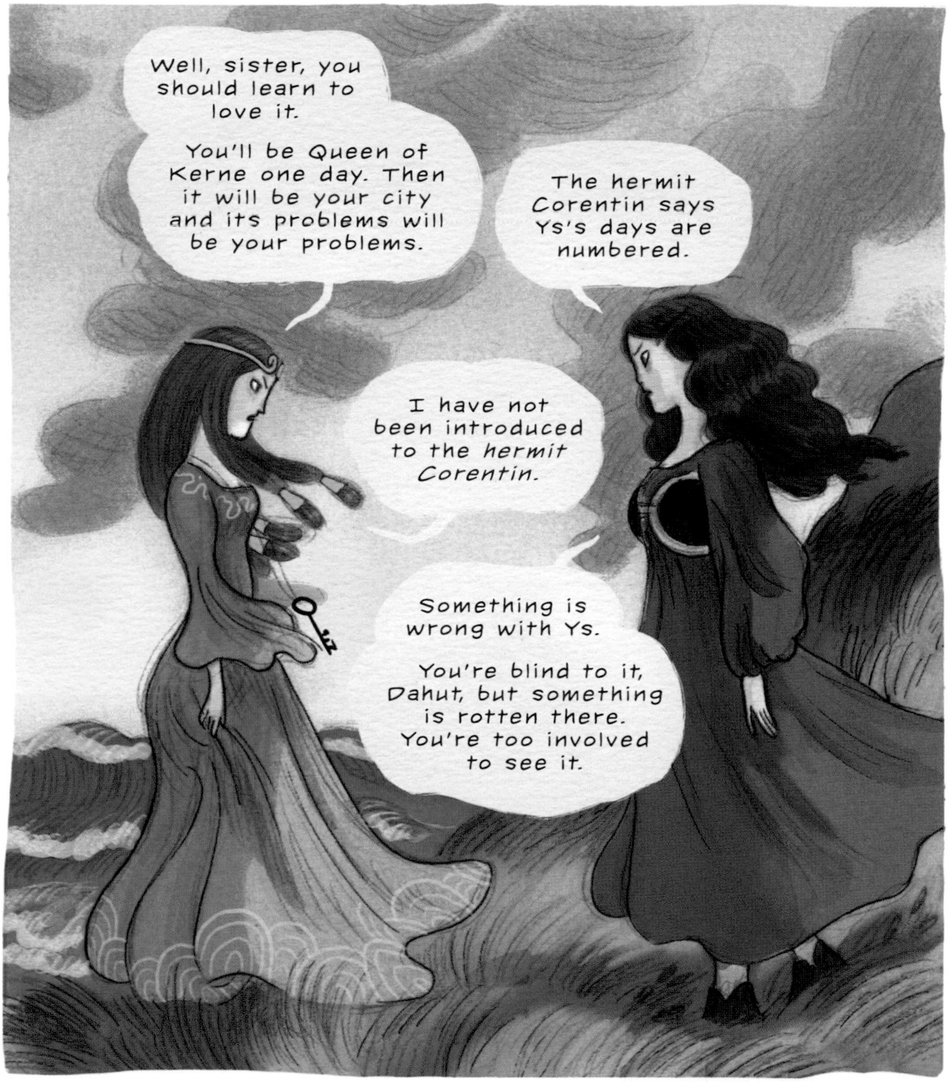

Well, sister, you should learn to love it.

You'll be Queen of Kerne one day. Then it will be your city and its problems will be your problems.

The hermit Corentin says Ys's days are numbered.

I have not been introduced to the *hermit Corentin*.

Something is wrong with Ys.

You're blind to it, Dahut, but something is rotten there. You're too involved to see it.

You think you are a fine and moral person, Rozenn.
I try to be—
But you're useless! There's so much to do—but you hide away on the moors and play with boars and never do the things that need to be done!
Oh? You spend your life at feasts and banquets.
And you go fishing with your fisherboy. Who does that help?

You know nothing, Rozenn, about what it takes to run an empire.
I have to do *everything*! You don't know—

What don't I know?

Who was that?
My sister, Dahut.

She's beautiful.

Almost as beautiful as you.

Ah!

A man's life is so fragile on the sea.
I am Rozenn's sister.

I saw you this morning.

You will see me often. We will be great friends.

You can ride a sea monster.
Only by dint of my great and sorcerous skills.
Otherwise, it would tear me apart. Would you like to try it?

Will you help me?

Mount in front of me. Leave your boat on the rocks.
You will learn a new way to fish.

Forward!

FWSHHHHH

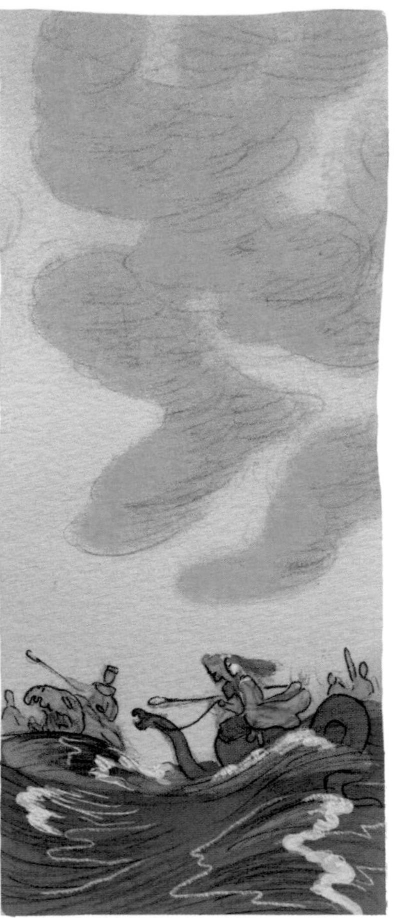

Were you sent by Dahut?

Yes.

What's your errand?

Come. See.

This is the best day!
Now you are a friend of both Rozenn and her sister.

If only the people from the village knew!
It would redound to your glory.

I find I do not want to take my arms from around you.
Well, I like them there.

Perhaps if you came back to my tower...

But Rozenn...

She won't know. She's off dancing in the bluebells.

Or weaving garlands for a civet cat.

What is...?

...My
blind cat...
Rozenn has
that bird
and it...
Are you sure
she won't find
out about
this?

I have to go. It's almost dawn. I have to find my boat.

If I could ask you a favor— I'm worried that Rozenn might see you.
It would break her wild little heart.

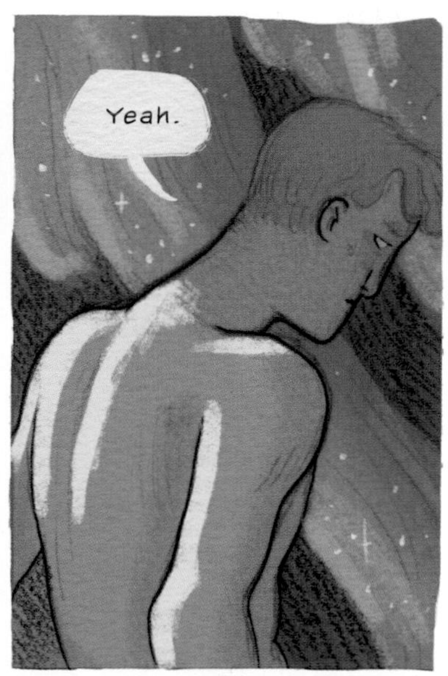
Yeah.

Perhaps you would wear...this mask?

We shouldn't have done this. I feel bad.

Your sister is a wonderful person.

Life is short, fisherboy.
We must grasp what pleasures we can.

Thank you, Princess, for your—
TAKE IT OFF. TAKE OFF THE MASK.

It's kind of stuck.

Take it off!

Mff! OW!

Ah!

Fine. I don't know what—

Get out. How could you betray my sister?

I don't believe you two!

No. What I did was kind.

rip

Always remember that: I was kind.

SHHHHHHHHHH!

DANG
DANG

FWSSH

You are welcome to the royal city of Ys, capital of Kerne, country of King Gradlon.
From what kingdom do you come?

Far away.

Have you come for business or pleasure?
Pleasure is business, and my business is pleasure.

I have come because someone with whom I have a contract missed a payment.
I have come to claim what is rightfully mine.

The king and his younger daughter, Dahut, will hold a feast tonight in the submerged ballroom.
I am sure you would be welcome.

I would not miss it for the world.

Welcome all. Outside, a tempest rages, but within the sea walls of Ys, we have light, and warmth, and plenty. Delight yourselves.
What else is there to do?

Who's the merchant? He has noticed you.
And I've noticed him. It is time for an introduction.

From a foreign land?

More foreign than you can imagine.

I have never been accused of lacking in imagination.
It must have been a long voyage.
No voyage is long when a maiden like you is at the end of it.

That was pretty.
But there are no other maidens like me.

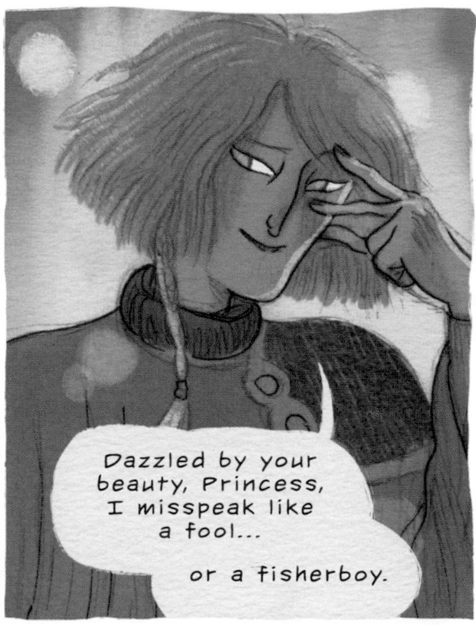

Dazzled by your beauty, Princess, I misspeak like a fool...
or a fisherboy.

SHHHHHHHHHH!

plip plip
plip
plipplip
plip plip

cheep?

chirp!
chirp!

Chirp!
Chirp!
Chirp!
Chirp!
What?

What is it?

Is there something unnatural about it?
Chirp! Chirp!

I hope they have closed the sluice gates.

Chirp!
What is it?
I'd better go down to see.

Down to the palace, Morvech. Something isn't right.

...So they slit open his stomach and nailed his entrails to a stake—then chased him around in circles, beating him with a club.

The entrails—they fell out on the ground—and as he ran, got wound up and wound up...
Which goes to show: You can't always trust your gut.

Ha ha ha!
You do know many curious and diverting stories.

Ah, you should have seen his face.

You were actually there?
I don't let anyone get the better of me. Like your princess here.

You're too kind, sir.
Am I? Not so much kind as already a little in love.

Are you? With whom?

I think you know.

Tell us another.

I knew a man once who ate his own family.

The sluice gates are closed. Nothing is out of place. Why do we feel so nervous?

clip clop clip
clop clip

Maybe Dahut will know if something's amiss.

Dance! Dance! In my land, we call it the dance of the Seven Deadly Sins!
Shake a leg, Master Gwencalon; you look as if you're Sloth.

Perhaps after this number, a private dance?
I would be delighted to enjoy a pas de deux.

At my tower, then.

Should I perhaps disguise myself so your good name won't be sullied?
With, perchance, a mask?

No... There is no need to wear a mask...

I don't wish you to.

TAP TAP TAP

TAP TAP TAP
TAP TAP
TAP TAP

It's just a merchant, little squeaker. What's the matter?
chiiirp!
chiirp!

The princess? She left a few minutes ago.

Dahut was just here...

She's over there with... Ah! She's gone, Your Majesty.

There is a fire in me I do not recognize.

Do you feel as if we have known each other before?

I admire your strength. We could rule a kingdom together.

We already do.
SNAP

Let that go.
Who did you say you are?

I am here because someone made a contract with me and my partners, purchasing our services, and then missed a payment.

Give me the key.

We are ready, in any case, to foreclose.

What power are you?
Our company is finished with this project.

I only missed one payment.
It is time to draw up the net and enjoy the catch.
Good-bye, Princess.

STOP!

KRRAKTOW

Hhh...
Hhh...

Heh heh heh. You cannot kill a snake with its own venom.

NO!
SLAM

BAM
BAM
Our partnership is not yet done! Tell me what I have to do!

SSSSSSSSS

Our business is concluded.
BAM
BAM
BAM

Rozenn!

To the sea gates! A traitor has the key! Rush!

HELP, CITIZENS! HELP! SOMEONE ATTACKS THE SEA GATES!

slip

Aaah!

CRASH
THUD

Hng!

CRANG

TAP TAP TAP TAP TAP TAP

HEY!
STOP!

shink

swk
swk
swk
swk
swk

Screeeee

CLANG
HSSSSS

Oh, God!

CLANG

CLANG
CLANG

CLACK

digga
digga
digg

Fwshhhh

HNG!
CLANG

Morvech! Kick down this door!

snort!

KA-PANNG

Forgive me.

Stop!

digga
digg

Haarg!

CRACK
Aeeh!

Back off, Princess Rozenn.
Let me destroy the evil your father and sister have created. This whole festering pit deserves to be washed away.

I'm warning you!

All you have to do to end the tyranny of Ys over the seas is to turn your back on all of this...

Just as you have every time before.

CRACK

Hhk...
Hrk...

What are you?

I am a gate.

digga digga
digga digg
CRR... CRRK
CRASHHHHHHH
God have mercy!

Hrrk!
Harr...

CRR
CRRACK

It's done, Princess.
The wicked of Ys will drown in their own city of sin. The stain of Ys will be washed from the earth.

Hsss!

stab

Aeeh!

HOOWOOOOOOOOO

WSSHHHHHHH

Daughter, what have you done?
What have I done?

My city...

I did exactly what you asked me to do!

Your mother's work... You've destroyed all of it.

By doing your work for you, Father!
The work of cruelty you were too weak to do yourself!
The city of a hundred spires...

Father! Sister!

Get on the horse!

CRASH

HOOWOOOOOOOOO

You're a demon, Dahut! There's a demon girl behind me! A devil!
What are you talking about?

Off, demon! Out, devil!

Stop! I was only what you wanted me...

...to be!

SPLASH

CRSHHH
HOOWOOOOOOOOO
WOOOOOOOOOOOO

It's all gone. I had it, and now it's all gone...
Where are we going?

Your old capital at Quimper. Where the rivers meet.

Rivers. I hate water.

I am sick.
My flesh is burning up, daughter Dahut.

I am Rozenn.
I am hungry. Bring me peacock and quinces.

There is a hut among those stones.
Perhaps someone could help us.

Welcome. You are not the first.

King Gradlon...

He is no king now. Perhaps tomorrow he will be once again.

I am hungry.
Bring me the flesh of the porpoise, so friendly to man.

I believe I could probably catch you a fish.

Here is a golden ewer from my feast hall.
Dahut, fill it with the finest Falernian wine!

You can fill it at the pond. Just scrape off the scum.

Are you going to catch and kill that poor fish again?

Living exacts such a high cost on us all.

Take as much fish as you want. It will multiply to fill you all.

What is this frogwater? Do you think I'm some beggar?
Just drink.

Ah!
It is warmed mulled wine with honey.

Hey. When we drank, it was just water.
Miracles have a dismal way of favoring the rich.

You! You aren't Dahut. You're Rozenn.

That's right, Father.

Dahut is gone.
Dahut, daughter of my crimes, dark pearl of my sorrow...

We all lost someone.

But I lost my daughter Dahut.

We are off to Quimper.

Farewell.

Corentin, holy hermit, you treated us with generosity when we had nothing.
Though you are a simple man, will you come with us and be installed as Bishop of Quimper?

Your Highness, I accept—if I might be fed on grains...and have a reflecting pool set aside for my fish, so he may at last live in peace.

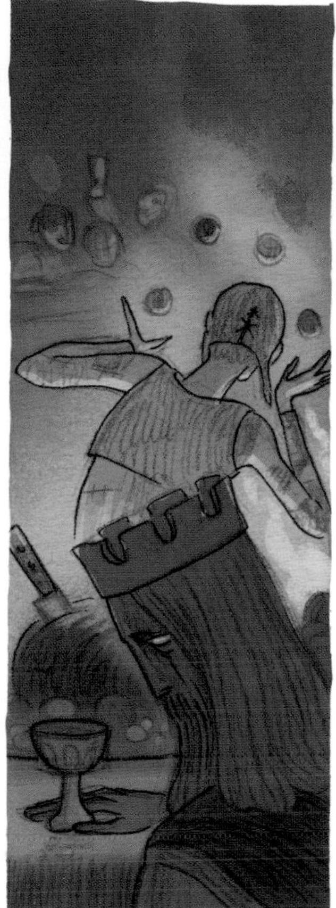

It's Queen Rozenn! It's the queen!

Rozenn!

Rozenn! It's so good you've come back.
My visit will be brief.

My love, I've been so sorry for how your sister seduced me.
I want to be your sure harbor.

You are as handsome as ever, Briac.

Everything is different now. We can build the world we dreamed of.

Yes. Everything is different now. Ys is beneath the waves.

And I am Queen of Kerne.

Once, my queen, on those cliffs, you said you could imagine courting a man with no royal blood in him.

Old rules need to change for new growth.

BAP

Why would I possibly forgive you, Briac the fisherman?

As my sister warned me, I must take up my mantle and be a queen.

I will marry as I need to—as the kingdom of Kerne requires—and I will rule.

This is where you used to come, Dahut, and sing and dance upon the shore. We made castles of sand and dresses of kelp.

What were we, Dahut, my sister? What might we have been?

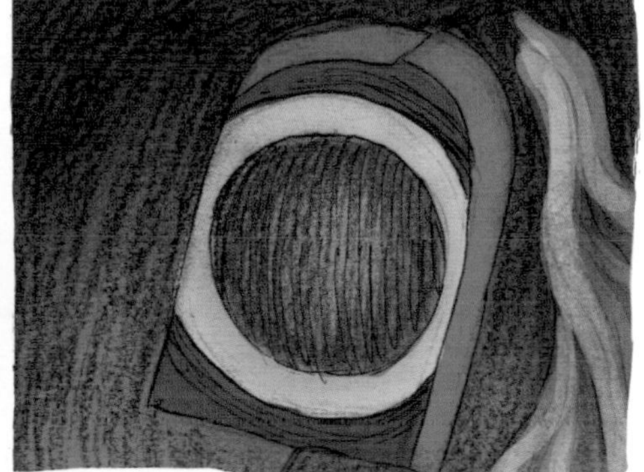

It has been more than fifteen centuries since Ys sank beneath the waves.

In Brittany, in the city of Quimper, stands the Cathedral of St. Corentin. Between its two spires is a statue of King Gradlon.

For many centuries, on feast days, Breton boys would try to climb up to give it a drink from an old pewter cup.
They threw the cup down to the crowd—and whoever caught it won a cash prize.

And on the farthest western point of Finistère—"the end of the earth"—where the Atlantic beats against the rocks, is the Bay of the Dead, where the bodies of Dahut's headless sacrifices were thrown into the waves.

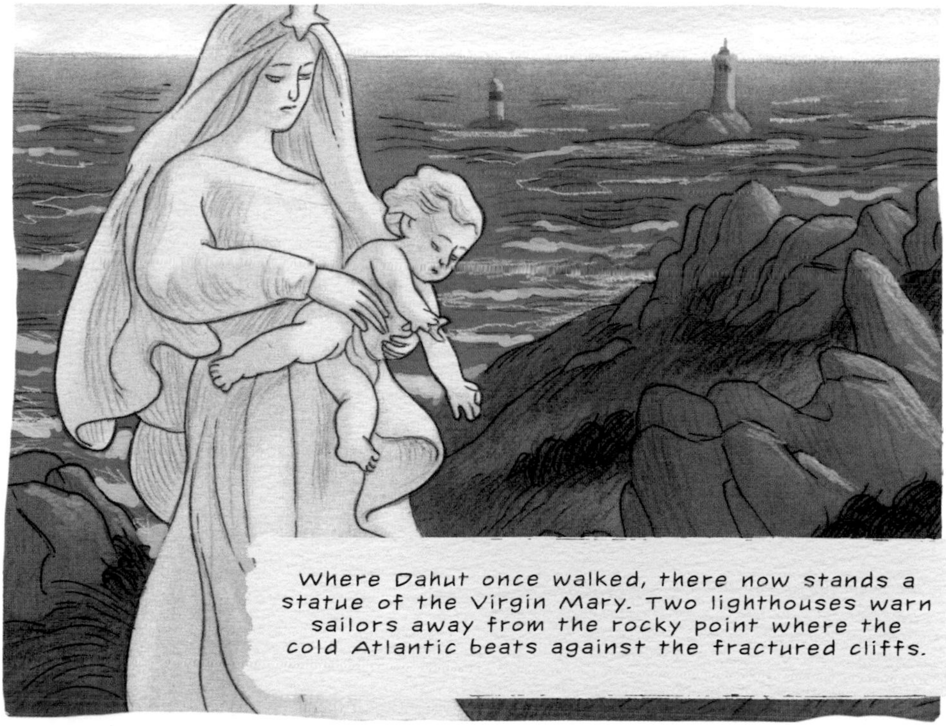

Where Dahut once walked, there now stands a statue of the Virgin Mary. Two lighthouses warn sailors away from the rocky point where the cold Atlantic beats against the fractured cliffs.

There is no trace of Ys, though sometimes fishermen say they hear the bells of the sunken steeples ringing in the deep, rocked by the tides.

Or the singing of a maiden
beneath the waves.

The Daughters of Ys is based on an ancient Breton folktale. Many different versions of this legend survive, but here are three (available online) that the author used to write this modern version:

Émile Souvestre, *Le foyer Breton: Contes et récits populaires* (Paris: Michel Levy Freres, 1874).
Édouard Schuré, *Les grandes légendes de France* (Paris: Perrin & Co., 1908).
Édouard Blau, libretto for Édouard Lalo's opera *Le Roi d'Ys*. Originally performed in 1888.

La Fuite du Roi Gradlon by Évariste-Vital Luminais (1884). Part of the collection at Musée des Beaux-Arts de Quimper in Brittany.